DEALING WITH BULLYING

BY HOLLY DUHIG

KidHaven
PUBLISHING

Published in 2019 by KidHaven Publishing, an Imprint of Greenhaven Publishing, LLC
353 3rd Avenue, Suite 255, New York, NY 10010

This edition is published by arrangement with Booklife Publishing.

Written by: Holly Duhig
Edited by: Kirsty Holmes
Designed by: Danielle Rippengill

Cataloging-in-Publication Data

Names: Duhig, Holly.
Title: Dealing with bullying / Holly Duhig.
Description: New York : KidHaven Publishing, 2019. | Series: Topics to talk about | Includes glossary and index.
Identifiers: ISBN 9781534526648 (pbk.) | ISBN 9781534526631 (library bound) | ISBN 9781534526655 (6 pack)
Subjects: LCSH: Bullying--Juvenile literature. | Bullying--Prevention--Juvenile literature.
Classification: LCC BF637.B85D84 2019 | DDC 302.34'3--dc23

Image Credits: All images are courtesy of Shutterstock.com, unless otherwise specified. With thanks to Getty Images, Thinkstock Photo and iStockphoto.
Front Cover – wavebreakmedia, prapann, Alexander Lysenko, Mc Satori, IB Photography, Maxx–Studio, Nata–Lia, Nisakorn Neera, Dragonskydrive,
nanantachoke. Images used on every spread – Red_Spruce, MG Drachal, Alexander Lysenko, Kues, Flas100, Kanate. 1 – wavebreakmedia, prapann.
2&4 – Liderina. 5 – gpointstudio. 6 – MPIX. 7 – Liderina. 8 – Imcsike. 9 – jannoon028. 10 – littlenySTOCK. 11 – Liderina. 12 – Fotokostic. 13 – Sergey Novikov.
14 – red mango. 15 – Deborah Lee Rossiter. 16&17 – Liderina. 18&19 – Rawpixel.com. 20&21 – gpointstudio. 22&23 – Rawpixel.com.

Printed in the United States of America

CPSIA compliance information: Batch #BS18KL: For further information contact Greenhaven Publishing LLC, New York, New York at 1-844-317-7404.

Contents

Words that look like **THIS** can be found in the glossary on page 24.

DEALING WITH BULLYING

My name is Rueben, and I've been bullied. Being bullied was horrible. It made me feel scared and very alone.

It all started when James joined my school. He had been <u>expelled</u> from his old school because he was misbehaving and didn't like being told what to do.

James started picking on me in front of my friends. He would call me names and kick my stuff. Everyone was scared of James, so my friends started picking on me, too.

NOBODY WANTED TO PLAY WITH ME ANYMORE.

Every time I got good grades on my homework, James would make everyone call me "teacher's pet." When I cried, he called me a crybaby.

ARGUMENTS AND BULLYING

Sometimes, friends have arguments. One time I argued with my friend Erica about what to watch on TV. She called me names, but she said sorry right away afterwards.

This made me feel sad, but it wasn't bullying. Bullying makes you feel sad for a long time. Bullying is when people do hurtful things over and over again.

JAMES USED TO SNAP MY PENS AND PENCILS EVERY DAY.

At School 🍎

I used to enjoy school, but James made me feel scared to go.

My School

Some mornings I felt really sick. I tried to tell Mom that I couldn't go to school that day because I was ill. She took my **temperature**, but I was fine. Not too hot, or too cold.

Mom asked me if I was worried about something, but I couldn't tell her about James. It felt too embarrassing.

I DIDN'T WANT MOM TO THINK I WAS WEAK.

Soccer and Friends

School made me miserable. The only times I felt really happy were on Saturdays when I had soccer practice.

The friends I have on my soccer team don't go to my school, so it's really fun! My next–door neighbor and best friend, Aaron, also goes to soccer.

AARON

TELLING A GROWN-UP

After a while, though, I couldn't even have fun at soccer.

I couldn't concentrate because I was busy worrying about school on Monday. My coach asked me if there was anything bothering me.

I told him all about the bullying at school. It made me cry. My coach told me it was normal to feel sad when someone is picking on you. It doesn't make you weak to ask for help.

He said I should tell my Mom or my teacher.

I AM BEING BULLIED

TALKING TO MOM

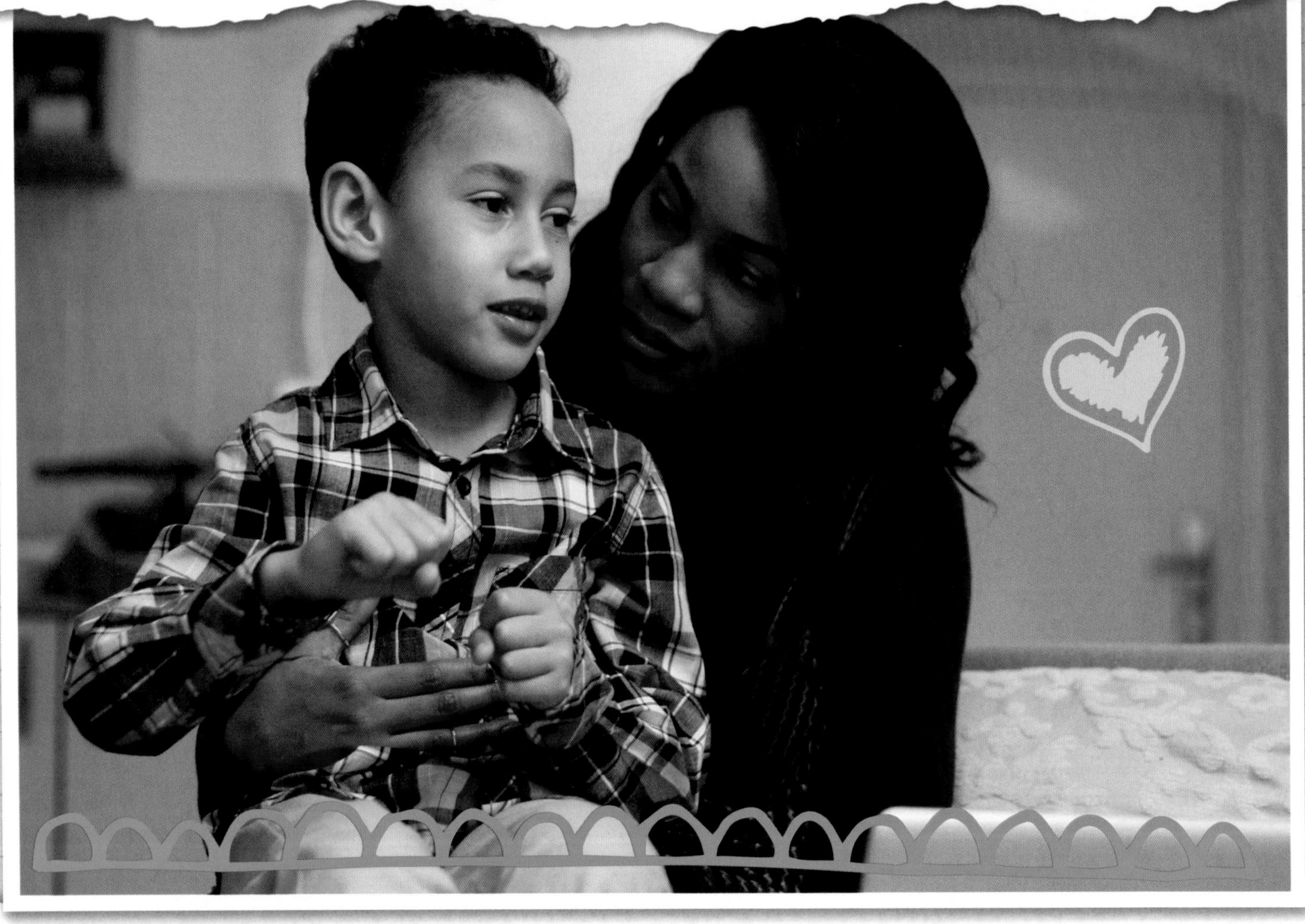

The next time I felt sick before school, I realized it was because I was scared of James. I decided to tell Mom all about what was happening at school.

Mom said I should make a list of all the things that James had done. This would make it easier to tell my teacher what had been happening.

TELLING MY TEACHER

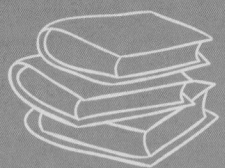

Mom came with me to tell my teacher, Ms. Hutchins.

MS. HUTCHINS

I was worried she wouldn't believe me, but she did.
She said she would talk to James and let him know that
bullying is <u>unacceptable</u>.

James had made me feel like it was babyish to complain about being bullied. It took a lot of **courage** to tell people about it.

Ms. Hutchins made James **apologize** to me for everything he'd done. I asked him why he chose to pick on me.

James said he was bullied at his old school for not being smart enough. He thought that if he picked on me, people wouldn't notice that he wasn't doing well in class.

I felt sorry for James, but it was still not fair to bully me.
I'm glad I stood up to him in the end.

WHAT I HAVE LEARNED ABOUT BULLYING:

- ALWAYS TELL A GROWN-UP
- IT'S BRAVE TO SPEAK UP, NOT WEAK
- BULLYING IS NEVER OK
- WRITE DOWN WHAT'S HAPPENING

I am much happier at school now. I have lots of friends because people aren't scared of James anymore. We know the right way to stand up for ourselves.

Glossary and Index

Glossary

apologize	to express regret for something you have done wrong
courage	being able to do something that frightens you
embarrassing	when something makes you feel awkward, self-conscious, or ashamed
expelled	no longer allowed to attend school
temperature	how hot a person, place, or object is
unacceptable	not allowed or bad

Index